Acknowledgements

This story came about from being a part of an online community on Twitter called 200 word Tuesdays. My husband joined the community first and spent a lot of his free time on there. I eventually got fed up of his attention being elsewhere that I decided to look into what was taking up most of his time. The idea was that a theme was set for the month and you would then write a small 200 word story to that theme or you could write a longer story and divide it into 200 word segments. There was a theme that caught my eye and so I wrote my 200 word segment but it wasn't a finished story. I was hooked. Over the course of the next few months I wrote more and more segments until my story had reached 26 parts which ended up tying in with a story my husband had written months before call 'The Mannequin' under the pen name of Lord Stabdagger. It is this story that I have included in my prologue with the permission of my husband. Unfortunately the group had to close but my story was still left at a cliff hanger that I couldn't get out of my head. I continued on the story in my own time over the course of the next year and a half until we have what is finished here. It may be a little hard to read in the 200 word switches between characters but I felt I had to continue it the way it started as my tribute to the 200 word Tuesday creator, Lara. I hope you enjoy my tale.

Prologue

For over forty years she stood in that shop window, adorned with the latest fashions and trends as the years rolled by. Her timeless beauty made her something of a celebrity with people from all over the world taking pictures, and keeping this humble little clothes shop in business.

She isn't just an ordinary mannequin, but an exact likeness of a young model who had a glittering career in the mid seventies. Isabella Chekronovski was a Russian beauty with jet black eyes and long golden hair. Fashion designers fell at her feet to model their creations, rewarding her with wealth, fame and attention reserved for royalty. She came from poverty to hold the world in her hands, gave generously to charitable causes, and was an inspiration to millions.

She had more than her fair share of romantic admirers, including Arthur, the owner of the shop. In the day he was a designer carving his own mark on the industry. It's said he fell so in love with her it drove him to the point of madness. He proposed to her but she politely refused, already engaged to a hunky American movie star. Arthur quit the industry when news came of the crash

As the world mourned the death of a celebrity couple, killed in an airplane crash whilst heading for their honeymoon, Arthur sold his part if the industry and opened a small shop with the likeness of Isabella in the front window. Over the many years only he would dress her. No one else was allowed to get anywhere near her. Every night he would take her from the window and lock her away safely in the basement. Many found it a little strange how he cared and protected the dummy as though she was a real person, often heard talking to her, kissing her lips, stroking her cheek, some joked he was married to a mannequin.

As Arthur grew old his model stayed young. All the way up into the last days of his life he kept people at a distance from her. Arthur and his eccentric ways held a warm place in

the hearts of all who knew him, the sweet
kindly old man who never married, devoting
his love for a window doll. His death
revealed a tragic, gruesome secret. Whilst
taking her to the basement, his heart gave
out. The mannequin lay broken by his side.
Contained within it, were the remains of the
woman who turned him down

By Lord Stabdagger

A case of the unexpected

Zoe

It was 6pm. Zoe was waiting by the clock tower in the market place as she usually did. It was unseasonably warm for an October evening even though the nights were drawing in. The pumpkins in the shop windows only added to the eerie atmosphere of the abandoned streets. Zoe felt uneasy at what she had to do; she had never gone back on a deal before. She had worked hard over the past 4 years to get to where she was today and her deals played a big factor in that. She had learned early on who to strike a deal with in order to make her task easier, but also knew that failure to deliver on her part would have serious consequences for everyone involved. It wasn't that she didn't want to deliver on her part of the bargain she had just run out of time.

Her mind began to race over what would happen next, every new scenario she imagined was worse than the previous. She contemplated abandoning the meeting, but she knew that wouldn't solve anything. They would still find her. Her eyes searched the deserted market place for signs of them approaching. All was quiet.

Travis

Travis refilled his coffee cup. There was a lot riding on tonight. He had the best people out in the field while he sat at his desk waiting for the news he so desperately wanted to hear. His whole career lay on the line. Travis had to admit to himself that when he first laid eyes on Zoe that he had his doubts. She was a scrawny, little scrap of a thing with glasses far too big for her eyes, but she came with very high recommendations and he had to admit to himself she had yet to let him down.

He remembered the first day he saw her; her flyaway hair, long, brown and curly secured with a black hair band, her ocean blue eyes and her school teacher style clothes. She could be attractive if only she made some effort. The glasses didn't help her looks either.

His phone rang; the noise shook him out of his reverie. This could be it; the news he was waiting for. He took a swig of his coffee, shifted in his chair and answered the phone. The voice on the other end was one he did not expect to hear from.

Mike

The gang were all assembled. Mike was ready and raring to go. This was his big chance to put an end to the rumour that he was not his father's son. After tonight no one would ever doubt that he had the guts to carry on in his father's footsteps; he was after all the eldest and now, therefore provider for his family. He wanted to make his dad proud. There was only one person who could stand in his way. Zoe.

Mike had always tried to abide by the rules like his mother had taught him to. She did not approve of her husband's trade but turned a blind eye as long as he brought in the money. She would plead ignorance as to where he had obtained his riches, putting on a good show for all of the elite women she spent her time with. She had grown accustomed to her lifestyle. With his father gone, Mike knew it was his turn to take up the reigns. Little did he know before he agreed to the task just how corrupt his father was. He knew he needed help to pull it off. That was where Zoe came in.

Rachel

She knew they would never get a chance like this again. If Zoe failed to gain their trust, the shadows would close in on themselves and immerse further into the darkness. Mike was the key; the weak link. If Zoe let Mike down, the rest of the gang would see his weakness and he would be thrown from their ranks. His position as ring leader is not as secure as he believes it to be. Rachel knew this. She also knew if Zoe failed tonight, the whole operation failed. What they needed, was more time. It had been 4 years since they have gotten this close to putting an end to it all;

unfortunately the ring leader was killed in the act, and the rest had gotten away.

Rachel searched the computer files once more. She was certain there had to be something she was missing. She was sure she remembered once reading a file about what happened that fateful night. Perhaps it was her imagination. She was certain none of those who had access to the files would remove it, so no such file could exist. But why, she asked herself, was she so convinced she had read it.

Frank

His worst nightmare was becoming reality. He thought he had solved the problem 4 years ago with the perfect solution. Now it was all coming back to haunt him. They were on his case. Frank knew he was toying with danger; it was the thrill of living on the edge that kept him going. He loved the adrenaline it gave him. He must act fast if he wanted to prevent discovery; a quick phone call ought to do the trick.

Frank knew the right people to call to get him out of his predicament; the problem was knowing what to tell them in order to get them to do as he asked. A request such as this is not likely to get brushed under the carpet so easily. He needed to choose the right target; the weak link in his chain; the only person who would do as he said without a second thought of the consequences. He drummed his fingers on his desk, turning the thought over in his mind. Where was his weak link? A sudden stroke of brilliance hit him; he knew exactly who to call. Without a second thought he picked up his phone and dialled.

Charlotte

This could be it. The moment she was waiting for. Charlotte had been staking out the market place for the past few weeks and so far came back empty handed. She had heard a rumour of where they met before their evening tirades, but had yet to catch anyone loitering about. She knew from experience that this was not the only meeting point, but without knowing their full schedule, she was left with no other choice. She had to choose one place and stake it out until she got the scoop of a lifetime.

Charlotte was an investigative reporter. She had been following the story of a gang for the past 4 years ever since her editor first assigned her the task of investigating why so many of the city's homeless went missing. Her first research task involved tracking the city's homeless and keeping a record of the numbers left on the streets. It seemed her editor was on to something; the numbers were decreasing while available accommodation numbers remained the same. She supposed that some could have migrated to other areas; that was until she saw them; the gang hanging about in the shadows. Her investigations led her here.

Zoe

Zoe had the feeling she was being watched. She looked ... she listened ... nothing there. This was the downside to her lifestyle; always having to cover her tracks to avoid her true intentions being discovered. It led to a certain amount of paranoia. She was good at what she does, but this particular deal was proving more difficult than she had originally anticipated. She relied heavily on the brains of her previous successes; Rachel. This was the first time the duo had come up short. Zoe couldn't shake feeling that someone was lurking in the background, always out of reach, ensuring their failure in this task.

This particular case had already surpassed her previous, taking 4 years to get this far and yet she still had mountains to climb before she could reach the end. Tonight was a pivotal point. She had to succeed. Just what she was going to say to them to gain their trust, she did not know.

A small movement caught the corner of her eye; a silhouette of a lone figure in the distance. She needed to know who else was lurking about tonight; an innocent bystander, or someone who could ruin the whole operation?

Mike

He thought about when he first met Zoe; she seemed the least likely person to be able to help him. Zoe didn't strike him as the kind of person to get on the wrong side of the law; that was why she was so perfect. With Zoe around people never suspected that he was up to no good; it was something he didn't have a lot of practise in with a mother like his. He had observed his father from a distance growing up and envied the ease in which he took control of a situation. That was Mike's downfall. He wasn't too good at leading others. He needed to prove to his father's former followers that he was ready to take charge. The way to begin was to discover the truth around his father's death and exact his revenge.

Zoe is a well connected individual. She has a certain knack for obtaining information. She had already managed to track down his father's movements from that night and had promised to help him find out who contracted the assassination; someone must be behind it. Why else would his father be killed when he was offering the deal of a lifetime?

Jerry

This was it; the night he would prove just how weak Mike was. The night they would stop playing their silly little games; Mike would be shown the door. If Mike refused to leave? Well they would just have to make him. Jerry would then be free to assume his rightful role and it would be back to business as usual; none of this revenge nonsense. The problem was Mike was a good kid. Too good. Jerry only allowed Mike to try, to set him up for failure, out of respect for Don. It was always Don's intention for Jerry to assume responsibility for the group, should the worst happen, and ensure his family was looked after in the process. He would never have dreamed one of his kids taking over. Celeste wouldn't like that. Jerry set Mike an impossible task for him to prove himself worthy of the role of leader, knowing he would fail and thereby honouring Don's wishes for his children to be kept out of this nasty business. The task was impossible for one reason; Jerry believed he already knew who was responsible and revenge on that person would put an end to their whole business.

Mike

He could see him looking; he knew Jerry expected him to fail. Mike would prove him wrong if he could. The last thing he needed was for his family to owe Jerry anything. Who did he think he was anyway? Some wannabe replacement father? Mike was the man of the house now; it was down to him to make sure they were provided for. Not his father's best friend. He supposed Jerry was only taking an interest to try and get into bed with his mother. He wouldn't be the first man.

Ever since Don passed, Celeste seemed to seek comfort in the arms of men or at the bottom of a bottle, rather than putting all her efforts into looking after the kids. Mike knew it wouldn't be long before they were broke if she continued down that path. Jerry seemed to be hanging around like a bad smell; giving his mother money towards maintaining their lifestyle. Mike had to wonder exactly what his motives were. That was why Mike wanted to take charge; to prove they didn't need to rely on the likes of Jerry.

Zoe had better deliver on her part. They could both suffer if not.

Charlotte

There she was again! Why was it every time Charlotte had been observing the gang, that woman showed up? Is she some sort of messenger for them, relaying messages from people they do deals with? Perhaps she was the puppet master; the mastermind; the one responsible for all their activities. She didn't look the type to be honest, but then again the best masterminds aren't always what we expect. If she was none of those things, then what was she doing there? She couldn't be a competing reporter; otherwise Charlotte would have known her. In a town this small the publishing house only possessed a handful of reporters; nothing like in the city where she moved from. Unless she was an out of town reporter; but then she would have seen competing articles.

Charlotte made it her business to check out competing papers to make sure she got the best scoop, and, if running the same story, she would find a way to get another spin on it. Perhaps she should start following this woman instead and see where it leads. Dammit! She's looking this way! If she's been seen Charlotte could lose out on the story. She better move.

Rachel

She knew she wasn't going crazy; she had read it somewhere. After traipsing through newspaper reports from around that time 4 years ago she found it. There was an article of a gang leader being shot 3 times in the chest and once between the eyes. It mentioned no names though. Rachel knew it had to be Don; it was all starting to fit. Mike insisted to Zoe his father was shot and here was a gang leader shot in the middle of checking cargo. There were no other gangs operating in this area as far as she was aware. What didn't fit was the coroner's report into Don's death saying he had died from a drug overdose. From the time Zoe had spent with Mike, there was no evidence any of them had any dealings with drugs. So why was that determined the cause of death?

Rachel looked at the newspaper article again; something about it sounded very familiar. She vaguely remembered a case of a 'John Doe' who had been shot. The man was never identified and no one was ever caught. She loaded up the police records once more and conducted a search on 'John Does'. Nothing.

Frank

Frank put the phone down. He had done it; it was easier than he had expected. One quick mention of Zoe and Paul was eager to please. Frank really detested men who got a crush on a girl out of their league, but it made them easy targets. He knew it wouldn't hold them off for long; he hoped though, that they may be held off long enough for him to get rid of it. How did he not see how close they were getting with their meddling? Being superintendent of the police force had its perks; connections in all the right places, power over others and the ability to tie up certain loose ends with a click of his fingers. The problem was Travis and his little team. He had underestimated how efficient they were and now the game could be up.

Frank hoped that by allowing the team to set up their little sting operation against the gang, they would find something to book them for and this time they would go to prison. The gang had become sloppy since Don was no longer in charge. With that woman going through old computer files, things were becoming tricky.

Zoe

The figure moved in the distance. She could see now that it was a woman; not only that, it looked like that new reporter woman. What's her name? The one who recently moved here from the city. Now what could she be doing hanging about at this time of night? Zoe had better check in with Rachel, see if she could shed some light on her. She picked up her phone. With a reporter hanging about, Zoe would have no choice but to put the meeting on hold; a story in the paper could lead to her true identity being revealed and the whole sting would be over.

Zoe checked in with Rachel first; it seemed this reporter had written a story about a gang leader being shot. Could it be that she instead could be the key to unlocking the secrets around the gang's activities? Zoe knew what she must do. First she needed to contact Mike and inform him the meeting would be put on hold. She could tell him the truth on this one; let him know someone was hanging about and so they were at risk of her overhearing, following them or seeing something she shouldn't.

Mike

Mike's phone rang; it was Zoe. She told him a woman was hanging about in the market place whom she believed could be the new reporter he had told her was doing some snooping. Man, he hated reporters. True he wouldn't have known the truth about his father being shot instead of dying from a drug overdose if a reporter hadn't been following his father at the time, but all in all they were a troublesome breed of human. He wondered where this would leave him with the gang. His deal had been broken. Mike decided perhaps tonight he should allow

Larry to take the lead in what they should do next.

Steering clear of the market place was a must; that much Larry made clear. He always believed that it was down to a meddlesome reporter that Don had been shot in the first place. The Keeper would not like a reporter in on their turf. Mike would just have to take a back seat tonight. He had failed. Well, not exactly failed, his deal was just delayed a bit. In the time he had got to know her, he trusted Zoe. Ok, maybe he fancied her

Travis

Travis put the phone down; Rachel had given him a lot to think about. It looked like they were barking up the wrong tree; if Zoe's hunches were correct, and Rachel assured him they usually were, Mike's father is the same gang leader that showed up dead in her previous investigation 4 years ago. There weren't just similarities between the two gangs like he thought. Zoe was right to all along, it was the same gang with just the son now in charge. Rachel had also uncovered an article that suggested that Don didn't die of a drug overdose. If that was the case then there was some foul play to be unearthed. Clearly the coroner either covered it up, probably due to having dealings with the shooting, or someone must have switched reports.

Travis set Rachel the task of finding the link. With the file of their 'John Doe' missing, it was beginning to look like someone had access to their server or there was someone inside their walls trying to hide something. Now the question remained; who could they trust? What exactly were the gang trading in if not drugs and who was paying them so much money?

Rachel

Rachel set to work. Her first task was to find out where the file had gone; a quick call to the technicians was in order. She picked up the phone and called Roy. Roy was always eager to help her; they went way back. While he searched the computer activity to find out the IP address of who last had access to the 'John Doe' file, Rachel set out looking at Don's record. Now she thought about it, it was suspicious why he had never served a day in jail when he had gotten so many cautions for thefts. Once would be a caution, a second or third time definitely meant jail. She looked at the names of the officers on those files; one name cropped up on a few occasions. Frank. It had to be a coincidence; surely the superintendent wouldn't have allowed a career criminal to walk free. He must not have checked for previous properly.

Her phone rang; it was Roy. He told her the computer activity showed that particular file had been accessed by an outside source. He ran an IP scan which appeared to lead him to Paul's computer. Frank's nephew. Now that was fishy.

Zoe

With task one out of the way Zoe set about achieving her goal for her second task. What was her second step? Well, that was to try and get the story out of this Charlotte as to why she is so interested in this gang and what, if any, connection they had to the report she wrote 4 years ago in the city. First she had to gain the reporter's trust. It is likely with her observing her from a distance that this woman believed Zoe to be a part of the group. She must convince her they were on the same side.

Zoe approached slowly; she indicated that she was unarmed and was not going to harm Charlotte in any way. She just wanted to talk. Knowing how reporters are eager to get the most exclusive scoop, Zoe promised that if Charlotte shared with her what she knew already about the gang she was so obviously following, then Zoe would ensure she got the story once the gang were brought to justice. In exchange Zoe wanted to ensure Charlotte wouldn't reveal to the group that she was actually an undercover agent. Surely, she couldn't say no to that deal.

Charlotte

She considered the deal carefully; it this was legit she would have story she had been chasing all these years. After talking to Zoe, she had no reason to doubt her and it explained why she had seen her about so often when trying to observe the gang. If she wasn't legit, well the game is up anyway, she had nothing to lose now. It was a no-brainer really.

Charlotte told Zoe how she came across the gang in the city when she was investigating the decreasing numbers of homeless as requested by her editor. She found the ringleader one night enticing 'ladies of the night', as she liked to call them, into a van. She observed the area that night and they were never returned. On another occasion she saw the same gang at the docks checking crates ready for shipping. On this occasion they also collected a briefcase. She thought she could hear people talking inside the crates but she wasn't close enough to investigate further. She suspected they were into human trafficking, but the night she thought she was finally going to uncover their trade, the ringleader was shot. She didn't see who did it. She fled.

Zoe

It was all starting to fit. The information Charlotte gave her was just as her informer had given her all that time ago. The gang, or shadows, as Charlotte nicknamed them in her article, were shipping crates, which Charlotte believed contained homeless people and prostitutes, and being paid for this. Now she had to catch them in the act. Charlotte had reason to believe that Mike, after seeking revenge, aimed to pick up where his father left off. Zoe suspected the death had to do with whoever paid them; with a reporter on the gang's heels, Zoe was sure it would seem the perfect solution to avoid discovery. Now the big question was, who was paying the gang so generously and what did they need with so many people? There couldn't be that much demand in a slave trade and if that was the case, Zoe was sure it would have come to light what the gang were trading in a lot sooner. So where were they being shipped off to?

Zoe knew Travis would want to hear what she had just found out; perhaps Rachel has managed to do more digging. They couldn't be far off a result now.

Travis

The plot thickens; a file deleted by none other than Frank's nephew, the gang trading in human trafficking with a mystery financer and yet the previous ringleader got away with so much. The deal Zoe was making may have been broken tonight but who would have thought it would have worked in their favour.

Rachel was starting to have suspicions about their superintendent, Frank, and to be honest, Travis could see where she was coming from. Right now though, he was not their priority. They needed to catch the gang in the act so they could once and for all put them behind bars and the town could feel safer. They could deal with Frank's leniency with Don later and why his nephew wanted that particular file deleted.

Rachel informed him that Paul was not one to normally do this, which was why she suspected Frank. Ever since Frank reunited with Paul's mother, he seemed to have some sort of hold over him. It was as if Paul was afraid of his uncle. Travis wondered whether Frank was somehow connected to the gang. Maybe they were blackmailing him; it wouldn't be the first time an officer fell prey to blackmail.

Larry

His orders were in; the Keeper wanted a delivery sending that night. The team had 3 hours to complete his order. This was going to be a tough one. There was nothing for it; an order like that could only be obtained in the city; only there, were there sufficient numbers to fulfil the Keeper's requirements. They must get to it. It had been 4 years since they had last retrieved their quota from the city; Larry supposed it must be safe by now to make a return trip. The order needed to be ready for shipping by 9pm tonight; the ship would be ready and waiting. Payment was to be collected tomorrow from their usual safety deposit box.

Larry didn't like the idea; they usually were given 24 hours notice before an order of this size and they always were paid the same evening. He had no other choice, though, they all had families to feed and with the reduction in orders lately, funds were running a little dry. Celeste wasn't coping well without her husband and spent a lot on drink. Not only did Larry have his own kids to look after but he had Mike's family too.

Rachel

Rachel's phone rang; it was Frank. That was odd; he normally spoke to Travis if he needed to inform the team of something. He told her that he had received a tip off that there was a ship coming into the docks around 9pm tonight and it was believed the gang would be loading their crates onto it. This was their chance to discover exactly what was in the crates. Rachel informed him she would get a stake out down there ready. Frank put the phone down. Was that a sigh of relief she heard? Frank certainly didn't sound his usual self; more on edge. Rachel felt a prickling sensation on the back of her neck. Her instincts told her he wanted them to stake out the docks to get them out of the way. She spoke to Travis; he agreed the situation sounded dodgy. He decided he would arrange a second team for the docks and that Rachel, Zoe and himself would obtain a warrant and search Frank's place.

He had been acting strangely recently; if Rachel's instincts were correct there was some link between him and the gang; a search would hopefully show them exactly what it was.

Dock stake out

There was movement in the distance; a ship had recently moored and crates were loaded onto the quayside. The tip off seemed to be correct so far. All they had to do now was too wait until the gang showed up and filled these crates with whatever cargo they were designed for. They still had an hour or so to go before the ship was due to set sail if the information they were given was correct. Mitchell poured the coffee while Jack broke out the sandwiches. Might as well refuel if they had a wait on their hands. This was the downside to stake outs, but it did carry a certain degree of excitement. Mitchell wondered how the others were getting on. Jack counted the crates; there were 12 in total. Whatever this shipment was supposed to be taking, it appeared to be a large order. He had heard rumour that Travis and the team believed it was people that were being shipped; there must be a lot of people if so. Then again if the original theory of drugs were correct then that too must mean a lot. A cargo of this size would surely be worth millions.

Zoe, Travis and Rachel

Travis jimmied the door; they were in. Now it was time for them to begin their search. They should split up; cover more ground. There was an awful smell coming from somewhere; you would think someone with a status like Frank would have made sure his home was presentable. There was nothing messy about the place exactly, but you couldn't ignore the smell. It was as though the house was rotting. Travis started in the living room whilst Rachel took the kitchen and Zoe the dining room. The place looked too neat for Rachel's liking; it was as though the house was barely lived in. The fridge didn't look stocked up enough for someone to be spending a lot of time there. Travis moved onto the office. He could hear voices from somewhere; it was as if they were coming from beneath him. He called the girls in. Zoe noticed the floor was uneven where the rug lay. They moved the rug revealing a door to the basement. With a nod to each other they lifted the hatch. The smell was overwhelming. Something was rotting down there; they were sure of it. One by one the team descended into darkness.

Frank

Frank turned down the single track road that led to his home; he needed to be quick. Rachel was a clever girl; he wasn't sure how easily she would have taken the bait. Rachel had been doing an awful lot of snooping this evening and it worried him how much she may have worked out. Who knew all that time ago when he first decided to assign the girls to Travis for this case, that they had a certain knack of finding information? He had always believed their success rate was down to the men that helped them in their cases. It looked like those two were actually the brains; the men must have just been the muscle.

As he rounded the corner, Frank saw the car. The jig was up. They were in his house; no time now to get rid of it. His only hope now was to give himself the best head start possible. Turning his car around as quickly as he could he drove off into the night. It was a good job he always carried a rucksack with enough resources in for a quick getaway. There was no time to lose. He had to disappear.

Dock stake out

A van was approaching in the distance. It was now 8.50pm. The tip off was paying off. By this time tomorrow the new reporter, as promised by Zoe, would be getting her police statement that the gang had been arrested and the town could sleep easy at night. Now they just had to wait for them to exit to get a positive ID and witness them loading their cargo.

The van pulled up; Mike was out first then Jerry. They opened the back doors of the van and began ushering a mass of people out of the back. The crowd was herded into the first crate and a second van pulled up. It appeared that the human trafficking rumour was correct. Mitchell looked through his binoculars and could see all of the people in the crate were chained together. There was a symbol on the crates he thought he had seen before.

A third and fourth van pulled in, even more people were being ushered out. All gang members were now accounted for. Jack gave the signal. Police officers swarmed the area; all hell broke loose. Arrests were made, while Mitchell set out about freeing the captives. It was over.

Zoe, Rachel and Travis

The first thing the team saw upon their eyes adjusting in the darkness was a mass of various tools lining the walls. It looked like there was some sort of work shop down here. Going further into the darkness, Rachel found herself walking into something solid. Travis found the light switch and a horrible sight met their eyes. There was what looked like blood splatters all over the place. In the middle of the room stood a large crate; many terrified eyes were staring back at them from within. Everything fell silent for a moment as the reality of the situation sunk in. This was no blackmail job; Frank must be the financer. Zoe gazed around the room; her eyes fell on a door to her right.

Inside there was a table with what appeared to be a mannequin on it; it was unfinished. Next to the table stood an old oil drum with what looked mysteriously like blood inside, among other things she didn't care to think about.

Rachel noticed something on the mannequin's neck; a maker's mark. This mark was familiar; this mark had appeared on the mannequin of a 70s supermodel; that ... turned out to be human.

8 months later...

Frank

Frank looked out of the cottage window at what was his new backyard. The trees of the surrounding woods provided the perfect cover from the outside world. He believed he would be safe to stay here, at least for a while. Providing his instincts were correct the trail was lost in Turkey before he boarded the plane to England and then drove the channel tunnel to find himself here, in the French countryside. He had been running a long time. He knew it would only be a matter of time before they pick up the scent again and he would be packing his bags, taking out his map and choosing his next destination at random. How long will it take for them to give up looking for him, he wondered. He supposed it all depended on how much they have unearthed since that night. He knew it was likely to be impossible to return for his daughter now. They have probably sent her away to be analysed; he had lost her again. He had to start a clean slate.

The alarm on his phone sounded. It was time to rinse out the hair dye, maybe then he could explore the village.

Investigating team

It was back to the drawing board again. Frank had given them the slip once more. Zoe took another look at the map where they had been tracking his movements since they discovered his dark secrets.

"There doesn't seem to be any pattern to where he ends up. It's almost as if he's picking destinations at random out of a hat."

"The question is what state of mind is he in and is he likely to try and pick up where he left off when he does settle somewhere?" Rachel enquired.

"Good job I've circulated his picture and the details of our investigations to other forces around the world then isn't it?" Travis chimed in.

"What on Earth was going through his mind to do something as sick as this? I can't believe I worked alongside him for all this time and never suspected anything."

"Zoe, he had us all fooled. He was the one who sent us after the gang in the first place." Travis reassured her.

"It's obvious why he did that now, isn't it?"

"Is it, Rachel?"

"Well it is to me. They were drawing too much attention to themselves. He needed them out of the way." Rachel stated.

Frank

Frank buried his head in his pillow and wept. He had lost his little girl all over again and it was eating away at him. His little Molly. He didn't even look like her daddy anymore.

"Daddy? Don't cry daddy. I'm here; I'm not lost. Are you going to bring me back some more dollies? Can I have a baby doll this time daddy? I have so many mummies and daddies but none of them have babies. They all would like some babies. I like you new hair daddy"

Frank lifted his head. He knew that voice anywhere. His little Molly; she was still with him. He smiled with glee. They could start over. Just him and his little girl. A clean start. He would have to change his identity again; he wouldn't want them to track him or he might just lose his daughter. What to call himself this time, he wondered.

"Daddy, I like the name William. There was a William in my class at nursery. Please change it to William."

"Then William it is my princess."

He picked up the phone and dialled. Tony was the only person he could go to now the police knew how Paul helped him before. He doubted Paul would want to help him now anyway.

Tony

"Hello?" Tony didn't normally answer a number he didn't recognise but then he knew not everyone had this number; there were not many people it could be unless it was telemarketing.

"Tony, it's me. I need your help."

"Fancy hearing from you, stranger. Last I knew you were all set up nicely in a big house and considered untouchable. Rumour is your now on the run... Well I know it's not exactly rumour you're famous now. You're all over the news... I take it this where my help comes in, is it?"

Tony listened intently on the list Frank was giving him. Should be easy enough to get a hold of what he needed. He sure knew enough people who owed him favours.

"Are you sure you're sorted out with accommodation. I know a guy who knows a guy who can get you this really nice big house with a lovely view. I know how you like plenty of space... Ok well if you change your mind you know where to find me. I'll need a week or two for your order... Ok let's say the 9th at noon, name your place... sure I'll be there... it's been a while since I visited there."

Tony hung up the phone. It was nice to be doing business with an old friend.

William aka Frank

The meeting was set. William was on his guard. He needed to be sure that Tony made good on his promise. It was all or nothing; either Tony came through for him again and William would be free to start over, or it would be a set up and he would face jail. William looked around; the area was filled with tourists. Les catacombes de Paris provided the perfect cover for the exchange and he hoped if things turned sour that he would soon lose himself in the crowd and manage to flee via one of the connecting tunnels. William had visited the catacombs a number of times in the past week and believed he had memorised the network of tunnels enough to make a getaway if it became necessary. The catacombs had a way of making him feel at peace and brought him and his daughter closer together.

"There you are, had trouble finding you with your new look. I don't like it."

"Tony! Aren't you a sight for sore eyes? Have you brought me my package?"

"Steady on there Will. Can I call you Will? Sorry but William sounds too posh, even for you." Tony patted the envelope in his jacket. "Got your package right here. Gonna cost you though."

"I wouldn't have expected anything less."

Molly

"Daddy? Have you got me any baby dollies yet daddy? You were gone a long while.

Please tell me you have a baby dolly for me daddy."

"Not yet, princess. I told you I needed to meet with Tony to get my name changed to stop them nasty people from trying to separate us. It will take time. I need to put my plan in place first. I won't be able to get you any babies just yet."

"You are going to try and get a baby for my mommy and daddy dollies aren't you daddy?"

"Of course, my princess. Don't I always keep my promises?"

"Not always daddy. You said you would get mommy to come home but she's not back yet. Where is mommy?"

"Daddy is still working on it baby. Those nasty people came and ruined it. We'll start over princess. You'll see when daddy gets the new place up and running and we get all the tourists, mommy will hear how well daddy is doing and she will be able to come home. I'm doing all of this for you. Now get some rest my little one and it will all fall into place soon."

William (Frank)

It was always the same routine. Every time he was gone for a while he would get the same bombardment of questions from his daughter, always asking the same thing, when her mommy would be home. He couldn't give his daughter the answer he wanted to give; in truth he didn't know whether indeed she would be home, let alone how long it would take if she did return. He could only hope that his belief that she would return if he could finally prove that he can provide for her enough would turn out to be true. Deep down he knew there was every possibility his wife would not return to him.

"Wallowing in your own sadness again are we Frank? Or should I now say William?"

William jumped out of his skin; he thought he was alone with his daughter. "Oh, it's just you. What are you doing skulking around Arthur? I thought I told you I needed time alone to plan out my next move."

"Oh, I'm sorry! Does my opinion not matter anymore? Who was it who told you that you could earn a lot of money through selling shop mannequins and such like? Now you want me to leave you alone! Don't you want my input on how we can get started on your museum?"

Investigating team

Zoe couldn't believe what she was seeing. The deeper she dug into Frank's background the more she realised no one really know him at all. She didn't know what was worse, the fact that he got away with so much for so long, or the fact that she was beginning to understand what could have driven him to such madness. She had no doubt about it that he must be suffering from some sort of mental illness. Surely no one is that evil through sane choices.

"Forensics are in, Zoe, that mannequin we found in the little girls room was definitely no ordinary mannequin."

"I half expected that result Rachel, especially after the thighs we found in the basement. Whether or not it was an actual mannequin was never in question for me. What's worse is I think I know who she was."

"You do? How?"

"Well I managed to do some digging and it appears that at one point Frank did indeed have a family."

"But his file said he was never married and there is no mention of any children. Are you trying to tell me that little girl was his daughter?"

"That's exactly what I'm saying."

William aka Frank

The idea swam around inside his head. How would he succeed in setting up a museum? However he achieved it he would need to avoid drawing too much attention to himself if he wanted a second chance at a clean slate. Maybe if could get his hands on the cargo from his storage crate he would have a starting point at least, but how can that happen without alerting the police of his whereabouts. He couldn't risk losing his daughter for a 3rd time.

Arthur was right. He needed help. Maybe he should give up his quest for fortune and be happy that his little girl has been returned to him. Surely he could just explain to Molly that her mummy has left them for good. She will get over it in time.

He needed some time alone to think. He had worked so hard for so long to try and win back his wife's affection so they could be a family again. Was he really willing to throw it all away now? He tried to remember the last time he spoke to his wife but all he could remember is her telling him over and over what a failure he is.

Investigating team

"Zoe I don't understand how can that little girl be his daughter? She only looks around 6 or 7 if that."

"She was 5 years old actually if my calculations are correct."

"What's this? Who's 5 years old?"

"Oh, hi Travis. Me and Zoe were just discussing that little girl 'mannequin' we found. Zoe reckons she was Frank's daughter."

"Impossible! Frank was nearly at retirement age. He's worked for the force for nearly 30 years and he's never had a relationship in all that time."

"It's not. Let me explain..."

Zoe recounted the documents she had been reading over the past few days. She really believed that she was starting to get some insight into how Frank's mind worked. Perhaps it was her mother's psychology influence that helped to gain some understanding but whatever it was Zoe couldn't help feel some sympathy for him. Of course some of what she was reading into his background is merely theory and speculation but the more she thought about it, the more her theory fit.

"Your theory is all well and good Zoe, but that still doesn't answer the most important question we need answered right now."

"Yeah Travis, I know, it still doesn't tell us where he is now."

Travis

Travis paced up and down in his office. The theory Zoe had just presented played on his mind. Could he really have missed how unstable Frank is? He had worked with him a long time but it was becoming more apparent how little he knew about the man. The thing that worried him most was how long Frank had gotten away with it all before being discovered. If Zoe's theory is correct he has been hiding this secret for a lot longer than they originally thought. Travis hoped she was wrong, but her instincts were usually on point. Maybe her thinking could be flawed on this occasion; distracted by her boyfriend, Paul. He is Frank's nephew after all and even he doesn't remember Frank having a family of his own. Then again if it did happen 40 years ago, Paul wasn't even born; it's possible his mother hasn't told him about them.

Travis hated this waiting game. They have already been trying to track him for the past 8 months and all they have achieved is dead ends and a potential new mystery. They were no closer to finding him than scientists were to finding the Loch Ness monster.

William (Frank)

Criticism from his wife rang in his ears. Remembering her always did hurt so much, especially when he wanted so desperately to make Molly happy. For years he catered to his wife's every whim but still it wasn't good enough. He never earned enough money; his business wasn't successful enough; he spent too much time at work. He couldn't win either way. It wasn't his fault he had inherited his father's debt along with the business, but he enjoyed his work too much to give it up. All that effort and he had to give up his career anyway.

His throat began to feel constricted and the cabin, once homely, became too small. He needed to get out; a change of scene to clear his head and catch his breath.

"Arthur? Look after Molly for a while won't you? Just popping out for a moment."

William stepped out of his cabin into the cool evening air, his feet taking him down a route he knew all too well. He returned to the catacombs in the dead of the night; being alone surrounded by death ignited an old flame. He felt his head clear at once. It suddenly became apparent what he needed to do. It was time to get to work.

Rachel

"Zoe, do you really think this Gordon fellow is our Frank? What makes you so certain?"

"Here, take a look at the news article that covered the fire. It states in the article that the whole family was killed in the fire but in the reports no bodies were recovered. When they were asking the neighbours for responses one of them said that they were told by Gordon himself that the wife had left him for someone else taking the child with her."

"Well it's possible she had second thoughts and came home."

"Yeah that's what I originally thought until I saw this."

Rachel glanced at the picture Zoe placed before her. It depicted a woman and child that were said to be killed in the fire.

"Oh, I see what you mean. That little girl is the spitting image of the mannequin we found. Do you think he staged his own death?"

"I do. I think he made it look like they all died to cover up the real cause of death of his daughter."

"Change his identity, move house, job done. Perfect cover for what actually happened." Rachel stated matter-of-factly.

"I'm hoping when I go with Paul to meet his mother tonight she might be able to shed some light on it."

"Try not to upset the woman."

Travis

Travis watched from his office as Zoe left hand in hand with Paul. Who'd have thought the two of them would end up getting together through all of this. Shame Paul didn't know his uncle all that well or they might have closed in on him by now.

"Rachel? What do you think of Zoe's theory? Do you think it's plausible?"

"I wasn't too sure but after seeing that photograph of the little girl that supposedly died in the house fire; I don't know what to think anymore. She is the splitting image of that girl from the bedroom. If it wasn't his daughter why go to all that effort to make a bedroom fit for a princess for some random girl you turned into a mannequin. This whole situation is the stuff of nightmares."

"If she is right it does tell us one thing though. It tells us he is not afraid to pack up and start somewhere new."

"Not to mention he probably has contacts to help him to change his identity."

"That too." Travis agreed. "This makes him even more dangerous than we initially thought. We need to find him and fast."

"We can only hope he slips up again." Remarked Rachel

"And not take 40 years before he makes another mistake." Travis added sarcastically.

Rachel

Rachel walked the short journey home from work. In just a few short months so much had changed already. No longer terrorised by gang members, children were finally allowed to play out. It started to feel like it was before all the trouble started. With the gang members behind bars the whole town was able to enjoy a clean slate. The park, previously always empty, was now full of life, even in this cool weather as families take advantage of a new found freedom. The revelations of the day played on Rachel's mind. If any of it can be believed then somewhere out there another town, village or city could be facing a threat much bigger than anyone could imagine. Rachel could only hope that Frank was too busy trying to evade capture to dare to continue where he left off.

There were so many questions left unanswered. If Frank and Gordon are the same person then why does Paul not know of this alternative identity? Of course it's possible he just hasn't been told. Maybe his mother is under threat. If the 'mannequin' they found is the girl from the supposed fire then what happened to that girl's mother? Is she also a mannequin that they just haven't found? Will finding answers to any of this help find him?

Zoe

Zoe straightened her skirt and took a deep breath. This was a big step for her, meeting her boyfriend's mother for the first time. She was afraid as she didn't want to upset her on their first meeting, but at the same time she had a mission in mind. She wanted to find out more about Frank. Try as she might to enjoy herself and have quality time with Paul, her mind couldn't switch off from work, not when he was out there somewhere. Failure was not something Zoe was used to. She also didn't want to upset Paul by quizzing his mother. She cared about him very much; she loved him. Of course the rumours went around that she was with him to try and catch Frank but they both know that wasn't true. The two of them had been trying to fight their feelings for one another since last year's Christmas party. At the time Zoe was with someone else who treated her badly and she loved the attention

Paul was giving her but it wasn't in her nature to cheat on a boyfriend. Fortunately for Paul, the ex-boyfriend didn't seem to share the same view and Zoe found him in bed with another woman merely weeks later. Paul had been a supportive friend to her ever since.

Paul

"Stop fidgeting. You'll be fine. My mother will love you just as much as I do, even if you do ask her about her brother."

"You knew I would want to ask her about Frank?" Zoe asked, surprised.

"Of course I knew! You've never been able to switch off from a case this big until it's been resolved. Why do you think I asked you to meet my mother? She already knows you want to know about Frank. Just don't make it the first question you ask her as she would like to get to know you too. Maybe wait till after dinner."

"Dinner? You didn't say anything about me staying for dinner. I would have changed if I knew."

"Don't be daft," Paul reassured her, "I think you look perfect. You always do. Just be yourself."

"Paul, you really are full of surprises. I don't know how to thank you for understanding my need to build up a background picture of your uncle."

"After I allowed myself to be threatened into deleting crucial files, it's the least I can do."

Paul grasped Zoe's hand and kissed it tenderly. He hoped his mother would keep her promise. She normally would never talk about her brother and he never dared to ask.

William (Frank)

William now had a clear idea of what he needed in order to start over. He left the catacombs and headed for home. His out of hours visit had gone completely unnoticed; he was certain that he must be the only person alive to know about that particular tunnel entrance. He wasn't going to let himself to get too comfortable in that conviction, however. One slip up and he could be facing the rest of his days behind bars.

He began making a list in his head of everything he needed to get started; hopefully Tony could deliver on it again. He would contact Tony when he gets back to the cabin. What would be the price this time, he wondered. As he walked back William noticed a young woman dump something in the top of a bin in a nearby alley before running away. Taking a detour he decided to check it out and found a small bundle of blankets in the top of the bin. He peered inside the bundle; this was perfect. The bundle contained just what he needed to make his daughter happy. The woman obviously wouldn't miss it if she went to so much effort to get rid of it. William scooped up the bundle and carried it home.

Marian

Today was a big day for Marian; she would finally meet her son's girlfriend. She knew instantly that she would like this woman. How could she not when she made her son so happy? Of course, her son had warned her that his girlfriend may want her input about his uncle Frank, which she was only too happy to share now. After hearing the antics her brother had been getting up to she only hoped that by the end of this meeting she could assist in any way towards his capture. Her only regret was not expressing her suspicions earlier but she had her little boy to think about and didn't want to put him at risk. Things would be easier now with him being grown up. If anything he was more at risk without that knowledge. If only he had told her he was being threatened, she might have been able to help Frank be put behind bars before he had chance to run away. Her only worry now was Paul's reaction to what she had to say. The recent developments only proved to Marian that her initial suspicions after Frank came back into her life were not misplaced. Her brother really was a monster. She now understood why her mother could leave him behind.

Tony

Tony settled into his chair for the evening. His recent meeting with William still fresh in his mind. Where did he get his ideas from for names, he wondered. William might be a name that was a damn sight better than Frank, but he doubted the name would fit in well with the cover France. True a few people chose to move there from the UK so he might get away with it, but if it was Tony's choosing he would have gone for a nice French name like Pierre. As if Tony's mind had been read, his phone rang; it was William. Tony had been expecting the phone call. If he knew the man the way he thought he did, it wouldn't take long for William to find that cabin too cramped. It was part of the reason why Tony promised him he would be able to secure a larger dwelling in the first place. He could do with William owing him a favour. That's what the two of them did for each other. Rarely did any actual money need to exchange hands between them. They had much more valuable things they could offer one another.

"Frank! I was expecting you to call. Too cramped already?"

William (Frank)

William growled with frustration. "Don't call me that! I told you my name is William now. Do you know how much trouble there could be if someone were to be listening in to the conversation. Not only would they track me but you would be done for aiding and abetting."

"Calm down William, my man, no one would be listening in to this conversation, I guarantee it. You know I am always careful. It's going to take some getting used to that's all." Tony explained.

William sighed to himself. He knew Tony was probably right; he was as slippery as butter when it came to being held accountable for his crimes. Tony was a professional. He's avoided detection for years. If anyone can help him, it was him. William explained to Tony what he required him to do and it was much more than just helping him to secure a larger dwelling.

"You do realise my price will have to increase with all these extras don't you?"

"I was counting on that. I'm hoping the extra cost may too help me with my venture."

"The museum? I see where you are going with this. In that case I definitely think we can strike some sort of deal. I'm in."

William put the little bundle he found into his freezer.

Paul

They had reached their destination. Ever the gentleman, Paul walked round to Zoe's side of the taxi to open her door for her before she had chance to reach for the handle. His mother always emphasised the importance of good manners to her son while he was growing up. Good manners cost nothing.

He knocked on the door of his childhood home and it was instantly answered by his mother. He could just imagine her pacing up and down merely minutes before their arrival and hovering by the door. She had been doing nothing but talk about finally meeting Zoe all week. Was she anxious or excited? That he didn't know.

Paul hoped that by his mother giving some insight into his uncle's past, it would give him some chance at redeeming himself; he did, after all put the whole case in jeopardy when he allowed himself to be threatened into getting rid of files. Zoe had forgiven him soon enough, but he was unsure of the views held by the rest of his colleagues. He deserved everything he got, even if he was just trying to protect the girl he loved. His fears that his uncle was serious looked to be well placed, however, with what they had discovered since.

"Zoe, meet my mother. Marian."

Tony

Tony put the phone down. The conversation turned out to be a lot more interesting than he imagined it would be. First thing first, Tony had to get his hands on the property he promised, and then he could focus on securing the cargo William wanted. Should be easy enough; he had the right connections after all. Now if he can manage to also stop the police from searching for William, it would also make his life easier. The deal he had just struck with William was too good an opportunity to pass up. For it to succeed 'Frank' needed to disappear from this world completely. Tony believed he knew the perfect way to make that happen. Just a few short phone calls and within the next couple of weeks, he could guarantee the police would no longer be looking for the man. There was no time to lose.

Tony picked up the phone and dialled his first contact. "Weasel, it's on. I need those keys by the end of this week ... The old man...? He won't be a worry either. I have plans for him. Can you do it...? Good. Get it done. Ring me when the house is ready... Yes! Of course you will be paid handsomely. The man is loaded. Keep me posted."

Stage one complete.

Zoe

Paul was right, Zoe got along with Marian very well. She needn't have worried about the meeting; they had been doing nothing but laugh all evening. Marian reminded Zoe of her aunt. It was nice to feel so comfortable around her, especially when things between her and Paul were starting to get serious. She hoped the conversation they were about to have wouldn't ruin the mood of the evening.

"Zoe, my son informed me that you wanted some insight on my brother. How about I get Paul to make us all a nice cup of tea and we can go into the lounge and I'll tell you what I know?"

"You're sure you don't mind talking about him? We don't have to if it makes you uncomfortable. I may be a chronic workaholic but I have a heart and won't force you to talk about him."

"Oh, don't be daft. It's about time I got this off my chest. I won't be able to tell you everything, mind, we grew up separately as children. He came back into my life around 40 years ago. I remember him being odd as a child but it was nothing compared to how uneasy he has made me feel since coming back into my life. He's not right in the head."

Travis

Travis slammed his fist down on the table. His frustration at not being able to catch such a dangerous man was amplified by the latest communication between forces. There was still no sign of the man in Turkey which was the last place they had managed to trace him to, and reviews of CCTV at the airports also turned up nothing. If he has left the country he most certainly had help to do so undetected. Just how many corrupt people were there in the world? This man certainly had a lot more connections than they had thought. From now on they had to treat anyone and everyone who may have had contact with him throughout his life with suspicion. The problem was how they could identify anyone who would be aiding and abetting the man when it was even clearer that no one really knew him. Would Zoe turn up something after talking with his sister? Travis didn't hold up much hope. From what Paul has already told them, Frank and his sister didn't really talk much. They were doing nothing but merely clutching at straws. How can a man whose picture is circulating worldwide remain free 8 months on? How much more chaos has he caused in that time? Travis poured himself a nice stiff drink.

Marian

Marian braced herself. It was time to face her fear and offload some important information about her brother. She only hoped that what she had to say would help lead them to getting inside her brother's mind and hopefully putting him behind bars where he belonged.

"You see, Zoe in order for me to make sense of it all I will have to start from the beginning. The man you know to be Frank did have in fact another name; the name I knew him by when growing up. He shared my father's name, Gordon -"

"You never told me Uncle Frank was actually called Gordon!" Paul interjected.

"Pipe down, Paul. I had my reasons. My mother and father never really got along for as long as I can remember. We were dirt broke and my father refused to look for other work. We were on the verge of bankruptcy. My mother found out where the money had actually been going. Turns out my dad loved the ladies of the night. She left him, taking me with her. Why she left Gordon I never knew. I suspect my father made her leave him there. He was never interested in me. Gordon was his golden boy..."

Rachel

Rachel sat alone in her flat reviewing her notes. This case had gotten right under her skin. She had not worked a file this big for a long time and she couldn't get it out of her mind. She needed a night out with the girls. She was getting too wound up by the whole situation and needed to let off some steam. It didn't help that she hardly saw Zoe outside of work anymore. She expected it wouldn't be long before she would be putting advertisements out for a new flatmate; she could see how serious Zoe and Paul were getting. Rachel sincerely hoped there would be wedding bells in the future. Zoe deserved to be happy.

Rachel put the television on; she needed to drown out the constant questions going round in her head. The anticipation of what Zoe might find out from Marian was too much to bear; they were clutching at straws and needed any help they could get to figure Frank out. Rachel was a bit of an amateur offender profiler. She studied psychology briefly before finding her calling as an investigator and found it helpful to try and get inside a suspects head.

William (Frank)

He couldn't wait any longer; he had the thrill of the hunt. It was no use waiting on

Tony; his makeshift workshop would have to do. He didn't know how long his prize would last in his freezer; anything could happen with a freezer that old. He cleared down the rickety table and got out the tools we would require. It wasn't his cellar but it would be sufficient for such a small project. For such a secluded area, William was surprised he was able to find the right sort of tools, and with those supplies he kept in the boot of his car when he fled, it was easy to get back to work.

He took out the bundle from his freezer; he would have to let her thaw out a little first. The anticipation of it all was almost too much to bear. Patience was the key for now.

"Is that going to be for me, daddy?"

"It sure is my sweetheart. Did you sleep well?"

"Oh, daddy! I had the best dream ever. Me and you were in this very big house, which was white on the outside, and it was completely full of my very own dollies in all sizes. It was like a big Barbie dream house."

"We will soon have that Molly. Very soon. Now, run along princess. Daddy needs to work."

Marian

"By the time I saw Gordon again, I had already had Paul and he had already changed his name to Frank. I never questioned it at first; he told me he changed his name because he was ashamed to share our father's name. I would have been ashamed too if I was in his shoes. Father had died a couple of years before I saw my brother again and left him to pick up the pieces with all of his debt. Apparently, father never did give up paying for prostitutes and had also turned to gambling after me and my mother left."

"So what made you think there was more to it all?" Zoe enquired.

"Well, when Gordon, I mean Frank, came back into my life he had nowhere to go and I let him move in with Paul and I for a while. You see, his house had been burnt down and from what he told me, his wife and daughter had died in the fire. I felt sorry for him. My only brother, losing his home and family like that. Well, one day, I was cleaning the house and decided to tidy up in the guest bedroom while he had gone out, and I found a picture of him with his wife and daughter..."

Zoe

"I don't understand. What was it about the picture that made you suspect he was telling anything but the truth?" Zoe asked. Her suspicions were being confirmed but she needed more proof.

"Ah, I knew that would just bring up more questions. It would be easier if I showed you."

Marian walked over to her desk and took out a family photograph and a newspaper clipping and handed both to Zoe. Realisation suddenly hit. She wasn't barking up the wrong tree at all. Staring back at Zoe from the photograph was the little girl that they had found in Frank's house and next to her on one side was Frank, minus a few changes he had obviously made to his appearance, and what she presumed to be her mother on the other side.

Zoe picked up the newspaper clipping perusing the article. The article was the same one she had been reading. The same photograph was pictured within it but without the father. It stated his photograph could not be recovered.

"He staged his own death?" It was a statement more than a question. "Do you mind if I keep these?"

"Go ahead; they are more use to you than they are to me now. Glad to see I'm not the only one who came to the same conclusion."

"Did you confront him about it?"

"I did ..."

Rachel

Rachel woke up with a start; she must have dozed off while watching the film. She couldn't even remember what she had been watching. She looked around the living room. Zoe was stood by the doorway trying to stifle down a laugh.

"Fly catching were we?" Zoe giggled.

"Oh, shut up." Rachel picked up a cushion from the sofa and launched it at Zoe. The cushion hit Zoe in the face and she soon stopped giggling "How long have you been home?" Rachel asked.

"Only just. It's been a very informative evening. Marian is lovely. She was as nervous to meet me as I was her. I think you'd like her. She couldn't tell us much about Frank as they were separated as children, but what she could tell us from when he came back into her life I believe will help us make sense of the man. Whether it will lead us to where he is now, I'm not sure. You're better at trying to find patterns in behaviour than I am. I can just read reactions."

"Well come on then, spill. I want all the gossip on him right now. This case has really gotten under my skin and I want to catch this bastard so we can go on with our lives again."

Travis

It was all too much to take in. Travis had worked with Frank for as long as he can remember; practically ever since he joined the force, and now here Zoe was telling him that Frank was actually called Gordon. Not only that, it was beginning to look like the man had killed his own wife and child to prevent his wife from leaving him. If he was so against his wife taking their child away, why on earth did he then go on to kill his own daughter. It just didn't make sense.

"Perhaps he didn't kill his daughter on purpose. Maybe it was just his wife he wanted to get rid of. Maybe the girl saw too much and he felt he had no choice. Perhaps someone else killed the girl or she died of natural causes? We're just assuming he murdered her." Rachel queried.

It was no use. They were going round in circles. They had been through all the what-ifs already. They may know more about the man, but they were still no nearer finding him. All it has done is open up a can of worms and left them with more questions than answers. They needed a breakthrough somewhere, but nothing added up. No patterns to indicate where he might be, or what led him down this path. The phone rang. Travis answered.

Zoe

The conversations of the past few days were taking their toll on Zoe. Even with a fuller picture, they were still no nearer. Zoe tried to listen intently on the phone call Travis was holding in case it was good news, but it's never easy when you only hear one side.

"Travis here... and you're sure there is nothing... No I appreciate it's probably been too long...Thank you. If you manage to turn anything up let us know. We appreciate you trying." He hung up. "That was the lab. They have run further tests on that mannequin and they haven't found any obvious cause of death. There is no evidence to suggest she was in a fire so looks like that was just a ruse. It's either been too long or the evidence has been destroyed in the process of preserving her."

"Another dead end then. Maybe we'd be better off if we closed our eyes and picked a place at random on the map, then one of go there and explore everywhere to see if we can find him." Zoe joked.

"Last time he sought out his sister when he was in trouble. Are you sure there is no one else he could seek out this time? Someone familiar? Someone he can trust? Another family member?" Rachel asked her.

"Marian said she was the only family he had left."

Rachel

Unable to make sense of everything they had found out, Rachel left the conference room and returned to her desk. She decided she would make a list of everything they knew so far. She worked better that way, making lists; it seemed to put an order on the events that had unfolded.

1. Frank was originally called Gordon. He was a family man who owned his own funeral business. This suggested the man was comfortable being around death which would explain his emotional detachment at being able handle bodies in such a way. He had grown up with it, carrying on the family business.

2. His wife was unhappy and had threatened to leave taking their daughter with her. They had gotten into a lot of debt not counting what

Frank had been left with when his father died.

3. His home and business were burned down in an arson attack, most likely set by himself or arranged by himself. This could be either to try get rid of the debt or to cover up the fact that he killed his wife by burning her remains.

Rachel had no doubt that something terrible had happened to his wife. They already knew his daughter had died but his wife has yet to be discovered dead or alive...

William (Frank)

William sat back and admired his work. It was by far his best one yet. Only a few more finishing touches were needed and Molly would have the doll she always wanted. It looked almost alive. He needed to take a trip to the village; the doll had no clothes. He couldn't very well give her to Molly like that. It was such a pretty doll. William almost couldn't believe that no one wanted her. He would get a bassinet while he was out shopping. No doubt Molly would want to play with the doll in a bassinet. Such a pretty doll deserved a bassinet, not a dumpster like where he found her.

William lovingly wrapped the doll in a blanket and placed her in his top drawer. It would have to do until he returned with the bassinet. He remembered Molly being that small. He wondered how, if things had been different, he could very well have been wrapping his own grandchild up in that blanket rather than a doll for his daughter who never had that chance to grow up. He knew he mustn't think like that; he had his little girl with him forever now. He wouldn't lose her to some man who might not treat her the way a princess should be treated. He enjoyed having his baby forever.

Zoe

Zoe glanced over Rachel's shoulder at the list she was writing.

"You're assuming Frank's wife is dead then? Is it possible that their daughter died of natural causes and they split up over him turning the girl into a mannequin and the wife ran off? I know it sounds far-fetched but then nothing about this case is normal."

"I doubt it. I believe he wouldn't have done that to his daughter without first practising the technique. Just look at her, he made her perfect. It almost looks like she could still be alive." Rachel replied.

"Are you suggesting his wife might be out there somewhere as a mannequin herself, like a practise dummy?"

"I don't know; just best not rule it out. Now go away you're ruining my flow."

Zoe left Rachel to finish her list in peace. It was an interesting concept. Could there be another mannequin out there with a resemblance to his wife? Is it possible after practising that he burned the mannequin of his wife in the house fire after? Zoe wondered whether it was worth circling his wife's picture asking if anyone had seen a mannequin like it; they would have to Photoshop the image first to give it the plastic like gleam they had witnessed of Frank's mannequins, but would it turn up anything?

Rachel

Rachel ignored Zoe's interruption and continued with her list.

4. Frank appears to be obsessed with things to do with death, even as a child. They found a collection of skulls and animal skeletons in his house and from what Marian told them he even collected these things as a child. He used to talk to the dead bodies kept within his father's morgue.

Maybe there were some underlying psychological issues there; beginnings of multiple personalities, perhaps, or just an overactive imagination.

5. He didn't appear to start killing for sport until after his daughter died or was murdered by either him or someone else. Carbon dating of the

mannequins recovered so far all correspond with this.

Could the death of his daughter have been the thing that pushed him over the edge? Why then would he turn to murdering innocent people for the sake of turning them into mannequins?

6. His father was an embalmer and his grandfather a taxidermist which was probably where he learned his trade. He was desensitized to being around bodies.

If he is obsessed with things surrounding death maybe that could give them a starting point. Maybe he will have chosen somewhere near attractions around death. It was a long shot, but it might work. She checked his previous destinations searching for a pattern.

Tony

Tony received the phone call he was waiting for. The property has been secured; now all that was left to do was for Frank to completely 'disappear'. That won't be very difficult. William will have his new residence by the end of next week and business will be able to carry on as normal. He couldn't wait to give him the good news. The cargo should be secured in a couple of weeks which will give plenty of time for renovations. Tony owed a lot to William. Their friendship was a mutual one which ensured they both stayed out of trouble; together they were untouchable. Who knows what they could achieve together next. Unable to contain himself any longer he picked up his phone and dialled.

"William, it's ready. I will have they keys tomorrow morning. Where do you want to meet? ... The Montparnasse cemetery...?

What time...? I'll be there. Are you ready to disappear for good? ... Let me know if you need a hand with the renovations ... I'll be in touch."

Tony hung up the phone feeling incredibly pleased with himself. William sure did have some curious meeting places, then again for a man who worked with death for so long, Tony was hardly surprised.

William (Frank)

William punched the air triumphantly; he would have his keys to his new residence tomorrow evening and set to work on his new venture. His fresh start will soon begin. He soon would be able to seal himself away from the world and look on from the side lines. At his age he didn't crave the thrill of a chase; he had become too cocky. It was time to take a step back and live out his days under the radar, and he knew just how he was going to do it.

William decided after settling in France that he must go back to his roots. There may not be a lot of money in being an undertaker, but one thing he could guarantee was he would never be out of work. He hoped that his new services he was intending to offer would give him the edge; the monopoly in specialist areas of honouring the dead.

He wasn't relying on that as his full source of income, however. He had his other business idea that he would run in the background. He was sure it would thrive; people had a natural curiosity for that kind of thing. The past few weeks visiting various attractions locally had proved that.

Paul

Paul shifted about uncomfortably from one foot to the other; his nervous energy radiated from him. Tonight was the night. He was certain of it. He had been deliberating over his timing for a couple of weeks but he couldn't hold off his urge anymore. He knew exactly what he wanted and he would just have to take the risk that the feeling was mutual. He would never know until he finally worked up the courage to ask. The scenery was just as perfect as he had imagined it and he only hoped that he would have the same response he had in his dreams. What would he do if she rejected his request?

It was too late to back out now; he could see her approaching. She looked stunning as always; her skin looked like it was glowing in the moonlight. Should he wait until after they had eaten or get it out of the way with?

He doubted very much he would be able to face his meal with the somersaults his stomach was doing right now. He hadn't given much thought into the timing during the evening.

"Zoe you look absolutely stunning." Paul pulled out her chair for her and gently pushed her under the table. He was ever the gentleman. Even in the moonlight he could see her blushing at his compliment.

Zoe

She never could get used to being complimented by Paul. Zoe always did have problems with her image, brought on by the selfish bullies she had gone to school with. She knew it was irrational but she still couldn't shake the insults she endured after all these years. She was plain; it wasn't exactly a bad thing but it wasn't glamorous either. It was one area where she and Paul's opinion would probably never agree.

Zoe smiled and turned a slight shade of pink, as she brushed her hair behind her ears, and gratefully accepted Paul's help with her chair. He seemed nervous tonight; it was like their first date all over again. She wondered what had gotten him on edge. Had his mother heard from Frank? Selfishly she hoped not; she felt like she really needed to shut off from work for a change. Finding him could at least wait till tomorrow.

To distract herself from her thoughts, Zoe picked up her menu and started to peruse her options for dinner tonight. She peered over the top expecting Paul to be doing the same, but he wasn't sat opposite her. Glancing to her right she saw him there, knelt down on one knee, a diamond ring in his hand. He barely had time to ask the question when she gave her reply.

"Yes!"

Tony

Tony put the finishing touches on the wreckage before him. Last night's meeting was a success. William would be busying himself with settling into his new accommodation by now; Tony knew how he didn't like to waste time. By this time next week at the latest, Tony predicted, Frank would no longer be on the list of wanted criminals and business could resume as normal. He had few doubts that their plan would work; William was exceptionally skilled.

The cargo William wanted would be arriving over the next few days. Tony was interested in visiting the museum William was planning when it was complete. The museum would be of mutual benefit to both of them; time would tell how beneficial it would be.

Tony stepped back to admire his handiwork. The scene in front of him looked dreadful; a good thing it did too, no one would bother digging too deep into it, hopefully. It was a scene that was best taken at face value. With the help of a friendly coastguard who owed him a favour, it will be ruled accidental. There should be no need for coppers to get involved, he hoped. As skilled as William was, he wasn't sure what the result would be if it was investigated too closely. Forensics might not be easily fooled.

Zoe

Zoe couldn't believe how much difference a week could make. She couldn't wait to get back to the office and share with everyone the news. She hadn't had chance to tell Rachel. Despite sharing a flat with her, Zoe hadn't seen anything of Rachel since Paul's proposal. The proposal was not his only surprise of that magical evening; he had also booked them a week's holiday behind her back and spoke to HR to get them to agree to give Zoe a week off. She had been working too hard and so the holiday was greatly appreciated, even if her usual rule was to not take holidays in the middle of a case. No one had expected that this case would take so long to reach a conclusion and she felt they were still nowhere near catching their man. Zoe hoped that they would have some good news for her when she got into the office. It would be the perfect ending to her week.

Zoe had a spring in her step as she made her way into the office that morning. Spying Rachel as she exited the lift she walked over to her, beaming. "Hi, Rachel, I have some news to tell you."

"We have news for you too." Rachel replied.

Rachel

"You should go first. If it's about the case then I want to hear it." Zoe told Rachel.

"I'm not entirely sure that you will want to hear this, but if you insist…" Rachel fixed Zoe with a look of warning that she wouldn't like what she was about to hear. Zoe nodded slightly in return. Oh, well may as well get the bad news over with, she thought to herself. "The case is now closed."

"What do you mean closed? Did you catch him while I was away? I was only gone a week." Zoe replied

"No nothing like that. It seems they have found a body and some coroner in the Turkish borders has identified it as our man. Some boat that looks to have run a-ground and caught fire was found and they say he was on board." Rachel handed Zoe the documents that had been received the previous day.

"Hmm, body mostly destroyed by fire; circumstantial evidence over the identity of said body. Sound familiar to you?"

"That's what we said, but the powers that be are having none of it. We have been told to drop the case. Anyway what's your news?"

Travis

"Ah, Zoe, you're back. Good. I'm afraid we have some bad news about the case." Travis interrupted, as usual entering the room at precisely the wrong moment.

"You're a little too late Travis, I've already told her. In fact you're just in time to hear Zoe share her news with us." Rachel interjected.

"News for us? Please tell us that this is all a joke and the case is still on and that the news is you've solved it" Travis added hastily.

It wasn't that he wanted the case to still be going on exactly, a detective always wants to see a case solved. It was more of the fact that both him and Rachel knew in their gut that the verdict that their suspect was now dead was complete hogwash. They had evidence to prove he had faked his death once before and no one was listening to the fact that it was very likely he had done the same thing this time. What was more frustrating than an unsolved case was a case that had the wrong conclusion. They will all look like idiots when it finally comes out that he was still alive all along and they failed to capture him.

Zoe

"No, that's not my news; it has nothing to do with the case." She was feeling slightly deflated after hearing the developments with the case that she was unsure she really wanted to share her news anymore. She should have gone first.

"Well? What is it? You can't come in here all bouncy, tell me you have some news to tell me and then leave me hanging." Rachel asked. She could see that Zoe was in a much lower mood than she had been when she arrived on shift. Well she did warn her to go first.

"Well... me and Paul ... Paul and I... well... we're getting married. That's why I've been away. I didn't know he had booked us a holiday so I couldn't have told you in advance but he thought of everything. We went out on our date as planned and he just asked me. I said yes of course, and then he sprung it on me that he had booked us a week in Paris."

The more Zoe shared her news, the more her good mood of this morning had returned. She detailed all the best bits of her holiday, not wanting to leave a single moment out. "Oh, it was so magical."

Rachel

Rachel leapt up suddenly and swept Zoe up in a hug, taking her by surprise. "I'm so happy for you. We deserve some happy news after all of this. Please tell me you're letting me organise the hen party."

Zoe giggled in response. "Like I'd have it any other way."

"I think I best leave you girls to discuss dresses and venues and flowers. Not like we have anything else to do right now. I'm glad something good came out of all of this; doubt Paul would have had the courage to tell you how really felt if this case didn't happen." Travis turned preparing to leave the room.

"Oh, don't worry, sir. We won't let this case drop completely. We're with you. We may not be able to spend all our time in the office on it because of the powers that be, but we don't give up do we, Zoe?"

"Nope, giving up is not our style."

Travis let a small smile play across his face as he left the room. He knew he made the right choice assigning those two to this case.

Rachel sat down with Zoe and asked her to recount the proposal and holiday once again, hoping one day that she would find someone as romantic as Paul.

William (Frank)

William took a step back to admire his
handiwork; the sign above the door finally
in situ read 'Musée des Morts'; Museum of
the dead. It was finally ready. It had taken a
mere three months for it to be up and
running once the cargo arrived. The thing
about the undertaker business was, if there
was no one dead then you had spare time on
your hands. That gave him plenty of time to
do up his new residence with a good lick of
paint and make it into a fine museum, with
his living quarters upstairs.

William had already made a name for
himself in the funeral business also. Who
knew that many people were looking for
more unusual ways to celebrate their dead?
It seemed people were getting bored of the
more traditional options of either burial or
cremation. He had made a number of
customers the past 3 months just by offering

services such as having the body buried in such a way as they will provide nutrients for a newly planted tree, or having a child's ashes placed into a teddy bear. He was hopeful that his new service that he was hoping to offer soon would take off just as well.

5 years later...

Travis

"Hey, Rachel look what just came in. A doll was going through customs, no one thought anything of it but the sniffer dogs were in operation that day and they freaked out."
"Why has that come through to us?" Rachel enquired

"Look, see the maker's mark. Does it look kind of familiar to you?"

"The mannequins we found? Don't tell me they now believe us when we say that he's still alive and now he's back up to his old tricks."

"Well... not exactly. They cannot prove that this doll was in fact an actual baby. It looks like it might just contain the ashes of the baby, but we have a lead. This doll was shipped from a place in France. Where did Zoe go on her holidays again?" Travis added excitedly. It was like every piece of the puzzle was beginning to fit together after 5 years of no leads and plenty of psychological profiling behind the scenes.

"France. But we can hardly expect her to go snooping. She's on holiday. Her first family holiday I might add; you know, with Paul and Amelia."

"Seems the psychologist was right though; he would want to seek acknowledgment eventually; he's slipped up. We can't miss an opportunity like this."

Rachel

Despite her better judgement, Rachel put the phone call in to Zoe. She didn't want to disturb their family holiday but she promised Travis she would try and find out if they were in the area. There was every possibility they were in the opposite side of France, in which case Travis agreed it would have to wait. Despite the suspicion around the doll coming through to their office the case wasn't officially reopened and so they still had to act under the radar. Rachel volunteered to go herself but Travis made it clear that he couldn't spare her at the moment. The only chance they had was if Zoe happened to come across him on her holiday.

To her relief, the call went to voicemail. For once Zoe must be doing as she was told and leaving her phone off as Paul had requested. Rachel smiled to herself as she hung up; she didn't really want to send Zoe there on her own. If this doll was made by him then they would get him when Zoe came home. Once the powers that be have looked into it they will reopen the case if it's needed. If he's cocky enough to use the same maker's mark, clearly he believes he's not going to get caught. He won't run yet.

Zoe and Paul

The sound of Amelia's laughter brought a smile to Zoe's face; this holiday was just what they all needed. Paul's mother had passed away at the beginning of the year and it had taken its toll on their family. Amelia missed her grandmother very much and didn't understand why she could no longer see her. They tried to explain to her that she was with the angels now, but the concept was a bit hard to grasp for a 4 year old. The trip to Disneyland Paris however, distracted her enough; it wasn't everyday you were able to meet Minnie Mouse in person. Paul was a like a big kid too, becoming over-excited chasing Amelia through the park. Zoe wondered how they would both handle it tomorrow when they leave and continue their tour of France. It was, after all, what Marian had wanted them to do with some of the inheritance; take Amelia to Disneyland, tour France and then scatter her ashes in the Atlantic Ocean.

They had made plans to visit the Eiffel Tower and to go to a museum which is said to explain death in simpler terms for children. Anything to help Amelia cope with losing her grandmother was worth a try, she reasoned.

William (Frank)

Molly squealed with laughter; William always loved the sound of her laughter. Everything had fallen into place; they were both happy again now even without his wife. Molly had started to accept that her mummy would never come home but that was fine. She had her daddy and space to play.

"Thank you for such an amazing doll's house daddy; it's huge."

"So glad you are happy my princess. Are all your dollies happy?"

"They are now that they all have babies of their own daddy."

William smiled as his daughter ran off to play. He finished his breakfast and glanced at his watch. It was time to open up the museum for the day. Business was going well. He had seen many families walk through his doors; it seemed a popular place to bring children considering the subject matter. Many believed it helped their children to come to terms with loss of a loved one. He should have done this a long time ago, but at the time when he first suggested the idea his wife had told him it was too morbid. Now he was proving her wrong. Maybe this was where the change had come from in Molly. She no longer asked when mommy would be coming home.

Rachel

Rachel knocked tentatively on Travis' office door. It was time for her to break the news to him that she had been unable to reach Zoe. He wouldn't be happy but she reasoned that once she brought him round to her way of thinking, he would soon see that they would eventually be able to get their man.

She entered slowly and started to speak but Travis cut across her before she could continue.

"Let me guess, for once Zoe has her phone off?"

"How...? You know what I was going to say?"

"I've never had you knock so quietly. It was as if you didn't want me to hear it. No worries. We will get him. He's being cocky; we just have to bide our time, I guess."

"This was what I was thinking. Besides its best if we do it when they reopen it, they'll soon catch onto the fact that we were right all along. I wouldn't want to send Zoe in there on her own. Paul wouldn't be of much use; he's terrified of his uncle. Besides do you really want Amelia caught up in all of that? She's only 4 and she's recently lost her Grammie."

"Yeah, you're right as always Rachel. It was a bad idea suggesting it."

"We'll get him Travis, trust me."

Zoe and Paul

"Are we sure we are doing the right thing bringing Amelia here? I don't want to upset her even more."

"I'm not sure I know what is right anymore Zoe, but we have to try. Who knows maybe it will help me with some form of closure. It's true what people say, we never talk about it enough that when the time comes it's this big scary thing to die. I've always had my mum there for me. Maybe if I didn't avoid the subject when she became ill I wouldn't have been so shocked when she passed. You told me I needed to accept that she was terminal. Now look at us. I've been a wreck and I think this week has been the first time I've heard Amelia laugh in months. I want this holiday to be closure, for all of us. We need to show Amelia that death isn't that scary. If this museum helps…"

"I know Paul; I just don't want things to get worse. Children don't come with a manual on how to handle these situations. You're right. You say your friend's brother said it helped his family. We'll try." Zoe grasped Paul's hand reassuringly and shouted Amelia to come off the slide. They purchased their tickets and entered the Musée des Morts.

William (Frank)

The day began like any ordinary day; just before 9am he opened the doors to the museum. It was so nice to see the place so busy. William didn't have much time to dwell on this fact however, as he had a meeting with a family to finalise their baby's funeral arrangements. He left his staff in charge of business while he saw to the parents of the deceased. Had he spent a little longer upstairs he may have not made the mistake he did later on that day.

The meeting lasted around an hour before he could finally get away and observe the happy customers to the museum. It was in the gift shop that he first saw her; his little girl. She looked even more angelic than he remembered. What was she doing down here? She should be upstairs with her dolls. He had not seen her as animated as this in years. Should he upset her and tell her to go back upstairs or let her play in his gift shop.

William approached her slowly and knelt down to talk to her. There was a look of fear in her eyes; she didn't trust her own father. He began to cry. "I'm sorry."

Zoe and Paul

Zoe searched frantically for her daughter; she couldn't have gone far. Amelia was too scared to be too far away from them. "Amelia! Where are you?!"

"She's over there! I see her! Paul elbowed his way past other customers in attempt to get nearer to his daughter, ignoring all the angry cries he got in return. "Get the hell away from my daughter you creep!" He quickly grabbed William by the scruff of his neck and dragged him away from his daughter's reach.

Zoe ambled over and scooped Amelia up into her arms terrified at the thought that she nearly lost her. It was a moment or two before she and Paul clapped eyes on the man he had dragged away from their little girl; he was sobbing. Surely Paul didn't grab him that hard. The man kept on apologising. Maybe the man was just trying to find out why Amelia was unsupervised; Paul might have over-reacted a tad.

"I'm so sorry Molly. I didn't mean for you to die." The man sobbed. He was inconsolable. Perhaps he had come to this museum for the same reason they had. Maybe he needed help dealing with the loss of a child perhaps.

"Did you just say Molly?" William lifted his head at the question directed at him. His eyes met Zoe's.

William (Frank)

Recognition suddenly dawned on his face. The moment he locked gaze with the woman cradling his daughter, he knew why the voice was so familiar. It was Zoe. The little girl in her arms wasn't his daughter; a look to his left at the man who had forcibly thrown him aside and everything fell into place. The little girl must be his great-niece. The resemblance to Molly was uncanny.

William knew there and then that the jig was up. He had finally been caught; he was finally going to answer to his mistakes. Even if he wanted to run he couldn't, the gift shop was so packed the two could split up and grab him easily. He would go quietly. It was actually a relief to not always have to look over his shoulder. His only regret was he knew he would lose his daughter for good this time. Deep down, he knew he already had but a part of him still denied that fact. He had lost her years ago; she was dead and there was nothing he could do about that.

"Stop talking nonsense. Molly's not dead, she's upstairs playing like she always does while we're working".

"Leave me alone Arthur. It's over."

Zoe and Paul

Paul held onto his uncle firmly while Zoe put the call in; it was obvious to him that his uncle had finally lost it. There was no fight in him anymore, and he had started talking to himself. First to an imaginary someone called Arthur, then his original name of Gordon, now William. Strangely none of these 'voices' scared Paul as much as it did when his uncle reverted into a child's voice. Clearly he had gone insane.

Zoe took Amelia outside while she phoned the office; the further she was away from Frank the better. He was beginning to scare Amelia with his constant ramblings to himself. Rachel answered on the third ring.

"Rachel, get Travis in there with you now and put it on loudspeaker so he can hear." She knew she must sound like a crazy person, not even giving Rachel time to speak, but thankfully Rachel did as she asked. They knew each other well enough to know when not to ask questions.

"Right I've got Travis here, you're on loud. Go ahead; tell us what all the fuss is and why you are ringing when you should be enjoying your holiday."

"I've got him! I've got Frank. Paul is holding him but don't worry he's coming quietly. I need you to make arrangements for deployment."

Rachel

She couldn't believe her ears. She and Travis had only just decided 3 days ago not to disturb Zoe's holiday and send her hunting for Frank and here she was ringing to say she had found him anyway. It was fate; they always said they were meant to solve the case eventually. Rachel listened intently on Zoe's recap of how she had caught Frank, better yet, it sounded like he was ready to confess all.

The two of them had only been discussing before Zoe left for her holiday, how Amelia looked like the 'mannequin' of the little girl they had found at Frank's place. So the 'mannequin' was his daughter. What had made him do that to her? They were not sure they were quite ready to find out; no matter how crucial it could be to the rest of the case.

Rachel left Travis in charge of notifying his superiors of the developments while she took care of the documentation for deployment. She wanted to get him brought back as quickly as possible and to relieve Zoe and Paul of the duty of minding him. She knew they could handle it, but her mind kept switching back to the affect it would have on her goddaughter. Where Amelia was concerned, Rachel was like a second mother.

Zoe

"Mummy, who was that man?" Amelia asked Zoe.

"Never mind my darling. He's just a bad man. Daddy and I just need to keep an eye on him until help arrives to take him home."

"Why did he say he didn't mean to kill me? What did he mean mummy?"

"He's just a very confused man Amelia. He will be gone soon and we can carry on with enjoying our holiday. We still need to send Grammie out to sea don't we. If you're lucky we might try and see if we can have one more day with Minnie Mouse before we go home."

This excited Amelia, her face lit up with a huge grin, no longer worrying about the strange man from the gift shop. Zoe watched her play in the park as she looked to see if there was any chance of booking another day's tickets at Disneyland. It appeared that all they needed to cheer up Amelia over the loss of Grammie was a day with Minnie Mouse. A sense of calm came over Zoe as she knew once and for all that everything will be fine. She hoped that Paul was feeling the same as he held his uncle securely inside, waiting for the reinforcements.

Paul

In what felt like no time at all the reinforcements arrived and led away his Uncle in handcuffs. He no longer felt like he had to look over his shoulder for the day that his Uncle would have shown up on his doorstep demanding help. Paul knew he was probably overreacting in his expectation that his Uncle would dare go anywhere near him but still had been unable to shake the feeling these past few years.

Paul stepped outside to find Zoe and Amelia; it was time to finish enjoying the rest of their holiday. It would be a busy time when they get back to the office on Monday as they start the process of putting Frank behind bars for good. Paul had a feeling, however, that it wouldn't be a prison cell that his Uncle would be getting contained in for the rest of his days; he belonged in an asylum.

"How are you feeling?" Zoe asked her husband.

"Better than I thought I would when I imagined this moment." Paul gave her a look that she recognised all too well; relief. He knew they would probably chat about it all later when little Amelia wasn't listening. "Come on let's find somewhere to eat, I'm starving."

Rachel

She had just finished on the phone to Zoe when Travis entered her office.

"Zoe just rang; she wants to know how we are getting on and if we have Frank already here. Typical of her, she just can't keep her head out of work can she?"

"Well come Monday she won't need to worry about trying to keep work off her mind. We will finally be able to make sure he never gets out again. It shouldn't be too hard; according to the officers who brought him in he's all too keen to make a confession. He keeps saying that his little girl wants him to. I think he's finally gone cuckoo; he believed Amelia to be his daughter. He doesn't remember his own daughter is dead." Travis replied.

"Thank god they got to Amelia quickly then or he might have taken her. I guess this

means he needs psychology assessment."
Rachel inquired.

"Already been in touch with the experts;
they will be here Monday also. We have
enough to hold him for the weekend before
we start the process of getting him
sectioned. Personally I would have preferred
him to have time behind bars but at least
either way he's secure and won't be seeing
the outside world again."

Zoe

"Well I have to say, that was an ending to
my holiday I hadn't expected." Zoe joked
with Rachel when she got back into her
office on the Monday morning. "What is this
I hear about another doll turning up while I
was away?"

"Ah, yeah. I tried to call you but you had,
for once, done as you had been told and had

your phone off. Travis wanted me to send you to investigate the source of the doll, but as we now know you happened upon the source by chance."

"Is it another 'mannequin'? He didn't make more out of human remains did he?"

"Well, not quite. There are human remains, but it's not what they are made of. The lab investigated it for us; turns out the doll is made from silicone but it is in fact made to be an urn containing baby's ashes. Apparently he's made these silicone dolls to look like the baby parents have lost and then fills them with the cremated remains. A bit unusual but still, honest work for once."

"I find that a bit creepy. Imagine me having a doll that looked like Amelia if anything had happened to her."

"I might remind you there is one that looks like Amelia purely by coincidence. Molly the mannequin."

"Don't… Just don't."

Frank's Confession

Travis, Rachel and Zoe

"Why are we even doing this? I thought the solicitor said that he didn't want us to record a confession from Frank on the basis that he is certifiably insane." Rachel asked.

"Well, the psychologist working with him has overruled. She thinks it is a necessary part of his healing process. She believes that he needs to do this if she is to get any further in helping him." Travis shrugged his shoulders. Personally he felt that Frank was beyond help. He had been having several conversations with the psychologist over the past few weeks and in his opinion nothing would work. As ever though, curiosity got the better of him and even he wanted to know what Frank had to say for himself, or rather to himself.

The trio glanced through the protective glass and saw Frank huddled in the corner rocking back and forth. They looked at each other with a mixture of loathing and pity on their faces. They hated the man for what he had done over the years but still, the humane parts of them couldn't help but feel pity. This was not the strong willed leader they once knew. He had clearly been suffering from mental health longer than any of them knew.

"Who is he talking to?" Zoe enquired.

Psychologist

"Himself." The psychologist said behind them. "Brace yourselves when getting the confession. This is where things really get confusing. So you brought the mannequin?"

"Yes, we brought her. It took a lot of convincing to get them to part with her for this I'll have you know. She is evidence at the end of the day."

"She is, or rather was, also his daughter. I know it's hard and I don't profess to understand everything, but you're intrigued into what he has to say, I believe this will help his healing process and this is the only request he had." She looked at the officers one by one hoping that they at least had the compassion to recognise that as horrid as the man behind the glass is, he is in fact an ill man. All of this could have been prevented had someone brought him to get help when he was younger.

"Does he still think she is alive?" Zoe asked.

"I'm not sure. I think it depends on which part of him is dominant at the time." She opened the door and let the trio inside.

The three settled themselves down at the table and set the mannequin down. As if a switch had been turned on, Frank stopped his rocking and made his way to the table.

Frank

Frank picked up the mannequin and held it tightly for a few minutes before sitting it in his lap. He looked across the table at the detectives opposite him.

"Thank you for bringing my little girl back to me. I thought I had lost her for good."

"I told you daddy, I'm not going anywhere. I'm right here." Molly answered him.

Frank shrugged this off and carried on talking. "I know I don't deserve your generosity at bringing her to me. I've been a wicked person."

"You've been more than that. Why not share with them exactly how wicked you have been? Why not tell them how you lost Molly and Vanessa in the first place?" William chimed in.

145

"That wasn't me, you know that wasn't me. It was 'Him'. I brought Molly back to us. She wouldn't be here if it wasn't for me. You know Gordon couldn't cope to do it. I made Molly happy; I gave her all her dolls."

"You didn't get mommy to come home though daddy. I do miss mommy." Molly interrupted.

"She was happy with me too, and she didn't need all those dolls you made. We lived an honest life unlike you, you con. Hiding behind your status thinking you were invincible." William added.

Zoe, Travis and Rachel

The trio looked on in confusion as they watched Frank talking to himself in front of them, his voice changing as he took on each of his different personalities. Had they not been warned prior to going in they would have found watching this man they once knew as their superintendent, talking to himself very disturbing. It still didn't make the interview that much easier. Zoe looked at the list in her hand trying to keep track of which personality they had already met and which one was talking to them at any one moment.

By far the most disturbing personality they had met so far was the one of Molly. Having a grown man talking to himself in the voice of a 5 year old girl was most unusual. Having that same man arguing with himself in different personas about which one of them made that same 5 year old girl happiest was even more bizarre.

Rachel wondered to herself who they meant when they mentioned 'Him'; the one responsible for what happened to his wife and daughter. As instructed though, the three of them did not interrupt him; doing so might ruin the whole confession, they just had to try and keep up with who was talking and what was being said.

Frank

"Will you two pipe down?! Arguing like a bunch of children over who made Molly happier. None of you did because she's dead. I was the only one who made her happy. I'm her father, not you pair!" Graham shouted. It was the first time he had been in control for a very long time. It was time they all accepted the truth. Molly is dead. 'He' killed her and now the rest of them were facing the consequences.

"Graham my boy! Good to hear you up and about. This is a wonderful surprise. You've finally stopped running away from the fact that they're gone. About bloody time, you could have saved all of this from happening you know."

"Now, Arthur we can't blame dear little Graham for everything can we? He didn't kill them." William piped up sympathetically. He felt sorry for the situation they found themselves in. It was the one they didn't like to talk about that caused all of this.

"We can. If he was strong enough then 'He' wouldn't have been able to get away with everything he did. You kept him out of the way these last few years didn't you?" Arthur continued.

"Will you all stop arguing? I don't like the arguing. Mommy and Daddy always argued." Molly cried.

Zoe, Travis and Rachel

Watching a grown man cry in front of them and acting like a 5 year old girl was surreal. They had now seen 5 of his personalities in fragments. The only one that they hadn't seen from the psychologist's notes was the one who committed the gruesome acts. The three of them looked at one another unsure of how to react. Should they try to question him and see if they could coax the confession out? They were told not to but they had been in the room for what felt like ages, watching the man argue with himself. It looked like they were getting nowhere with it. Neither one of them seemed to know the best way to respond while Frank just sat opposite them sobbing like a child, clutching the mannequin like it was his toy doll. It made them uneasy.

They could see the man in front of them unravelling. In this uncontrollable state neither one of his personalities appeared to be the dominant one. He was switching between them rapidly and it was becoming harder and harder for them to keep up.

With uncertainty of the best course of action, they just sat quietly and waited for him to continue, neither one of them willing or comfortable with the idea of offering him comfort and reassurance.

Frank

The sobs soon turned into an evil cackle; the man looked at the detectives in the eyes. There was wildness about them; something evil lurked under the surface. There was a shift in the atmosphere as the evil within made its way to the surface.

"Don't you all understand you're all weak? You all let me in. All this bickering amongst yourselves; there are better things to do. You all act innocent but you're all obsessed with death just as much as me, with your funeral homes, experiments in plastination and museum of death. I just like to deliver it. Frank, you wouldn't have made the mannequins if I didn't provide you the materials. William, you wouldn't have started offering the service of those urns if you weren't so disgusted at what Frank did. I made all of you what you are and yet you shunt me!"

"No you're just the murderer!"

He began his evil laugh once more; eyeing the detectives, he licked his lips in anticipation. Frank leapt across the table and took hold of Travis' throat and began to strangle him. Zoe and Rachel struggled with Frank to get him to release Travis; the door opened and two orderlies ran in and quickly sedated him. The three detectives left the room taking the tape recording with them.

Zoe, Travis and Rachel

"Are you ok Travis?" Rachel asked

"I'm fine. Let's go. I think we have all we need to put this case to bed. He clearly has gone off his rocker."

The three of them started to leave the building when they were called back by the psychologist.

"I'm so sorry. Every time I've interviewed him, that personality has remained dormant; they only ever referred to him as the murderer. Had I known he would come to the surface, I wouldn't have sent you in there."

"Don't worry about it. He wasn't gripping too hard. I think part of him was still trying to fight that personality. We have what we need." Travis reassured her.

"Aren't you forgetting something? The mannequin? Don't you need her back?"

"What good will it do now? He may as well keep her. He may have a monster lurking inside him but we don't." Travis answered.

"We'll clear it with the office. They have the evidence they need. If she can bring him some happiness in his insanity… well he may as well keep his daughter." Zoe added.

The three of them left knowing that they were unlikely to see Frank in the outside world ever again. They took comfort in the fact that it was finally over as they walked out the door.

Zoe

"Still no change?" Zoe enquired as Paul walked through the door. He had been once again to the mental health hospital where his uncle had been sectioned to visit him. It had been a couple of weeks since his confession.

"No. They tell me he doesn't talk to anyone. None of the psychologists can get through to him or help him. The only person he talks to is Molly, if you can even call her a person.

154

He has tea parties with her everyday they tell me. Why did you all decide to leave Molly with him? Surely she should have been laid to rest properly. Aren't you breaking the rules?" Paul wondered.

"No. Travis cleared it with the courts. She may have been a victim of manslaughter, but at the end of the day she is his daughter and as mentally unstable as he is, he is the only one left who can decide how he wants her to be remembered in death. We're not monsters. He clearly has remorse for what happened to her as that it was tipped him over the edge completely. We just chose to show some compassion and let him keep her. He was a good superintendent before he lost control and his obsession took over." Zoe shrugged.

Paul

Paul looked at his wife, tears threatening to fall from his eyes. He could understand now why they did it. It was just as he felt. His uncle may have done terrible things but he was in no mental state to have controlled his actions. That was why he still visited now and then. He was still his flesh and blood and truly the only family that Frank had left aside from Amelia and there was no way Paul would risk taking her there with him especially with the resemblance she shared with Molly. Still, he couldn't leave Frank to fester in that hospital completely alone with no visitors for the rest of his life. He still felt an odd sort of duty to him. At least having Molly kept him happy, maybe one day he would finally come back to reality.

Paul could never begin to imagine how his Uncle ended up spiralling out of control but the psychologists suspected it all began with his upbringing. Constantly being around dead things and being ignored by his father, it became a sort of obsession for him. It is unclear whether he would ever be able to have a normal life ever again. Whether Paul would continue to visit his Uncle, he didn't know. Only time would tell.

Printed in Great Britain
by Amazon

60860961R00092